Text copyright © 2025 by Hà Dinh
Jacket art and interior illustrations copyright © 2025 by Yong Ling Kang

All rights reserved. Published in the United States by Random House Studio, an imprint of Random House
Children's Books, a division of Penguin Random House LLC, 1745 Broadway, New York, NY 10019.

Random House Studio with colophon is a registered trademark
of Penguin Random House LLC.

Visit us on the Web! rhcbooks.com

Educators and librarians, for a variety of teaching tools, visit us at RHTeachersLibrarians.com

Library of Congress Cataloging-in-Publication Data is available upon request.
ISBN 978-0-593-71178-1 (trade) — ISBN 978-0-593-71179-8 (lib. bdg.) — ISBN 978-0-593-71180-4 (ebook)

The illustrations were rendered in watercolor and colored pencils, with digital editing.
The text of this book is set in 15-point Garamond Premier Pro Medium.
Interior design by Rachael Cole

MANUFACTURED IN CHINA
10 9 8 7 6 5 4 3 2 1
First Edition

the JADE
BRACELET

by **HÀ DINH**

illustrated by **YONG LING KANG**

RANDOM HOUSE STUDIO ⌂ NEW YORK

To my beloved mother,
who lives on in my heart and in my stories.

And to all the women and girls around the world.
May our stories continue to be cherished in our memories,
remembered in our writings, and shared
with children for generations to come.

—H.D.

On my birthday, Má hands me a present and tells me about one of her favorite traditions.

"Bà Ngoại gave me one when I was little. Now it's my turn to give one to you," Má says.

Bà Ngoại was Má's mom. She moved from Việtnam
to live with us after Ông Ngoại passed away.

She would sing sweet lullabies and snuggle with me
at night. I loved hugging her arm until I fell asleep.
Then one day, she fell sick and left, too.

I wish I could hug her again.

"What is it?" I ask Má with my hands clasped together.

"It's a jade bracelet," Má says.

My eyes look at the bracelet.

"It's so green," I say.

"Jade is a special green rock. Every girl in our family has her own jade bracelet. Jade is precious. Jade is rare, and jade is magical. Just like you are to us," Má says, looking into my eyes.

"Did Bà Ngoại have one when she was small?" I ask Má.

"Yes, and she wanted me to give one to you," Má says.
I look at our family altar and see Bà Ngoại smiling at me.
I nod my head, and Má takes my hand and slides the
bracelet onto my arm.

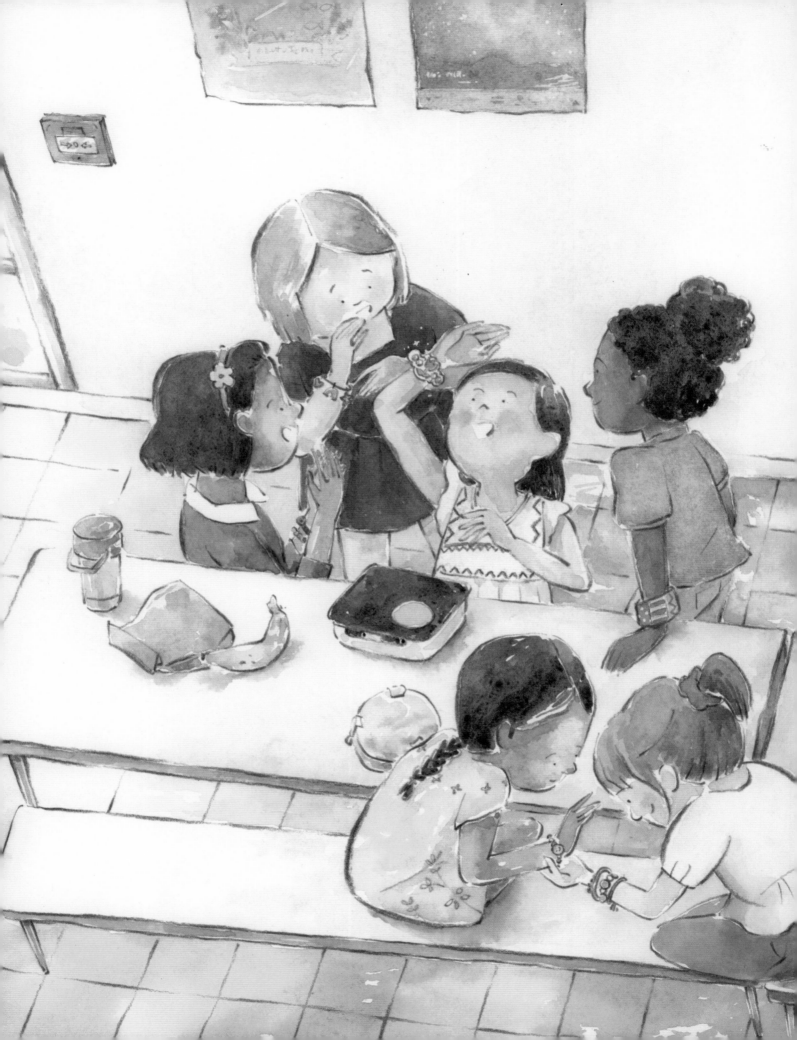

The girls at school wear bracelets, too,
but theirs are not like mine.
Theirs have butterflies with fluttering wings,
crystal charms that sparkle with glitter,
and colorful beads that glisten like rainbow pearls.
They talk about them in the hallway.
They show them off at lunch.
They even trade them at recess.
"My bracelet shimmers in the light," one girl says.
"My bracelet sparkles in the sun," another brags.
"My bracelet shines even in the dark," another boasts.

I wish I loved the jade bracelet.

I wish I believed in its magical powers.

Mostly I wish I had magical powers to make it disappear.

All I have is
a green,
plain,
hard-as-a-rock bracelet
that doesn't
shimmer,
sparkle,
or shine.

Two days pass, and no one notices my bracelet at school.

But today is Picture Day, and Má has other plans.

When it's time to take my picture, I shuffle my feet and stand on the big X on the floor.

I hope no one sees this ugly thing, I think.

I try to pull the bracelet past my knuckles, but it's stuck.

"Now leave your hands at your sides," the photographer says.
My cheeks turn warm, and my hands are clammy.
"That's a beautiful bracelet!" she says.
A wave of whispers rushes through the line,
and everyone's eyes fall straight on me.
"Smile!" the photographer says, and the flash lights up.

That afternoon, I run from
the school bus to my room.

With a strong tug, the jade bracelet
slides off, and I toss it on the floor.

"I don't want this bracelet!" I cry.

Tears fall down my cheeks as my words burst out before I can stop them.

Má kneels down and gently grabs my hands.

"Why do you say that?" Má asks.

"It's just a green rock!" I say.

"It's so much more than that, Tiên. It gives you good luck and keeps you safe. But most importantly, it's the spirit of the women who have worn a jade bracelet in our family, including Bà Ngoại.

"They are watching over you," Má says.

"But I want what the other girls at school have. Their bracelets have colorful beads that glitter and shine. Mine is plain and dull," I say.

"Yours glitters and shines, too. You have to look closely to see it," Má says.

I stare at the bracelet lying on the floor.

"If you don't like this bracelet, we can get

you the one you really want," Má says.

We go to the store together
to find the bracelet that has butterflies
with fluttering wings,
crystal charms
that sparkle with glitter,
and colorful beads
that glisten like rainbow pearls.

"Is this what you wanted?" Má points at the bracelet I have dreamt about.

My eyes shine looking at it.

It's as perfect as

the ones I've seen

and as beautiful

as the bracelets other girls wear.

But deep down inside,

I know

it isn't as perfect

as the one that

Bà Ngoại wore.

I hesitate and look at Má.

"Let's go home," I say.

Back in my room, I think about Má's words.
I look at my jade bracelet, and for the first time,
I see it sparkle and glisten in the light.

The next day, I tell my friends about my jade bracelet in the hallway.
I show it off at lunch.
A girl even asks me to trade it with hers at recess,
but I remember Má's jade bracelet
and the warmth of Bà Ngoại's hugs.

I cover the bracelet with my right hand
and squeeze it tightly
as if I were hugging Bà Ngoại again.
"This one is for me to keep," I say with a smile.

Everyone's family has traditions.

Some help us remember the past.

Some honor where we came from.

Some are celebrated out of love . . .

. . . and this one is now my favorite.

AUTHOR'S NOTE

This story was inspired by a jade bracelet that my mom gave me when I was seven years old. Like Tiên in the story, I didn't fully understand its importance, and I even wished for a bracelet that looked more like those of my friends. However, I recognized how special it was to my mom. I decided to wear it to honor her and stay connected to my family with such a meaningful symbol.

Eventually, I outgrew my jade bracelet, but my mom treasured hers and wore it until the day she passed away. To continue this beautiful tradition, I gifted a jade bracelet to my daughter when she turned seven. I wrote this story as a love letter for my mom and a gift for my own daughter, Tiên.

Every now and then when I see fellow Vietnamese women wearing jade bracelets, it reminds me of my mom and the traditions and appreciation of our culture that she instilled in our family. The jade bracelet will always have a special place in my heart.

This is one of my older sisters and me, celebrating Easter. I'm wearing the yellow áo dài and my jade bracelet.

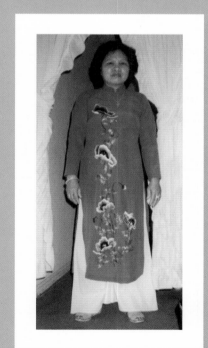

This is my mom and her beloved jade bracelet.